"Fire! Fire!"
Said Mrs. McGuire

Written by
BILL MARTIN JR

Illustrated by
RICHARD EGIELSKI

Harcourt Brace & Company
SAN DIEGO   NEW YORK   LONDON

Requests for permission to make copies of any part of the work should
be mailed to: Permissions Department, Harcourt Brace & Company,
6277 Sea Harbor Drive, Orlando, Florida 32887-6777.

Library of Congress Cataloging-in-Publication Data
Martin, Bill. 1916–
Fire! Fire! said Mrs. McGuire/Bill Martin, Jr;
illustrated by Richard Egielski.
p. cm.
Summary: In this version of the old rhyme the fire turns out
to be the smoke from the candles of a birthday cake.
ISBN 0-15-227562-2
1. Nursery rhymes. 2. Children's poetry. [1. Nursery rhymes.]
I. Egielski, Richard, ill. II. Title.
PZ8.3.M4113Fi 1996
398.8—dc20   94-11258

PRINTED IN SINGAPORE

B D F H J K I G E C

The illustrations in this book were done in gouache on 300 lb. watercolor paper.
The display type and text type were hand-lettered by Judythe Sieck.
Text type was set in Schneidler Medium.
Color separations by Bright Arts, Ltd., Singapore
Printed and bound by Tien Wah Press, Singapore
Production supervision by Warren Wallerstein and Ginger Boyer
Designed by Judythe Sieck

For Randy and Cindy Methven
—B. M.

For Michelle, Gina, Jen, Paula, Amanda,
Alex, Nicole, Lauren, and Emily
—R. E.

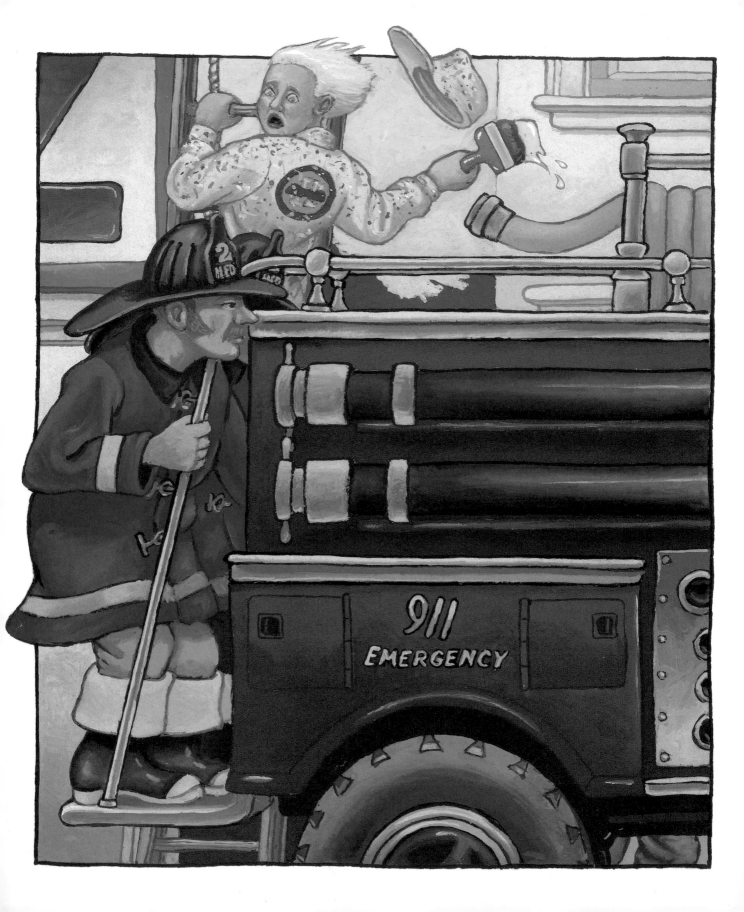

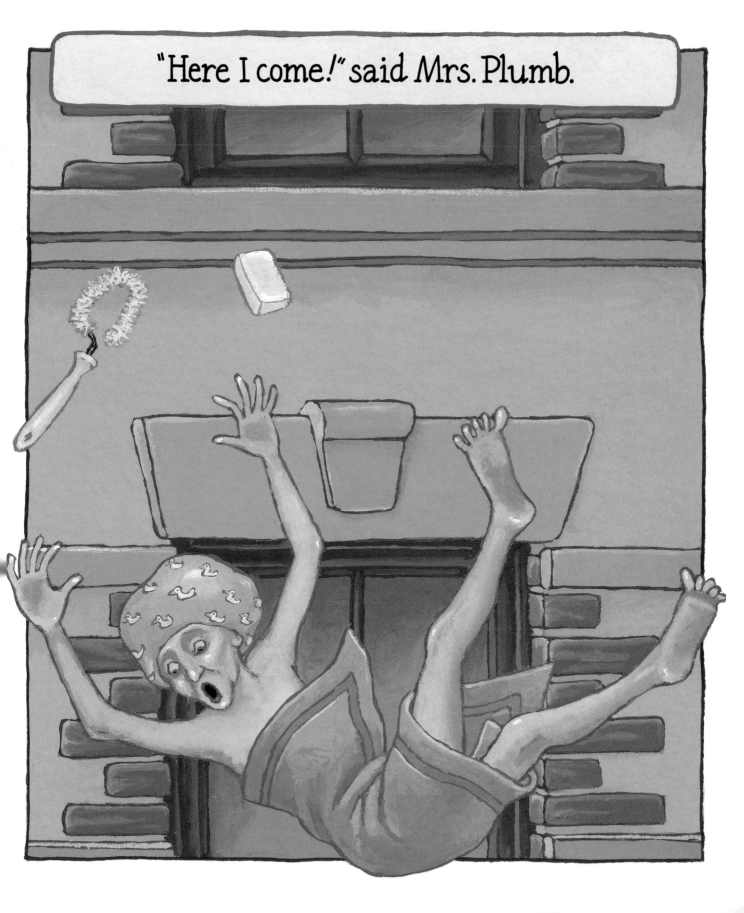

as she slid down the stairs with a sack of potatoes.